TWENTIETH CENTURY FOX PRESENTS IN ASSOCIATION WITH MARVEL ENTERPRISES, INC. A 1492/BERND EICHINGER PRODUCTION IN ASSOCIATION WITH CONSTANTIN FILM "FANTASTIC FOUR" IOAN GRUFFUDD JESSICA ALBA CHRIS EVANS MICHAEL CHIKLIS JULIAN McMAHON KERRY WASHINGTON MUSIC BY JOHN OTTMAN MUSIC SUPERVISOR DAVE JORDAN FILM EDITOR WILLIAM HOY, A.C.E. PRODUCTION DESIGNER BILL BOES DIRECTOR OF PHOTOGRAPHY OLIVER WOOD EXECUTIVE PRODUCERS STAN LEE KEVIN FEIGE PRODUCED BY CHRIS COLUMBUS BERND EICHINGER AVI ARAD RALPH WINTER

MARVEL 1492 PICTURES WRITTEN BY MARK FROST AND SIMON KINBERG AND MIKE FRANCE DIRECTED BY TIM STORY

SOUNDTRACK AVAILABLE ON WIND-UP RECORDS

www.fantasticfourmovie.com

Library of Congress catalog card number: 2005921618

Book design by Joe Merkel

1 2 3 4 5 6 7 8 9 10

❖

First Edition

www.harperchildrens.com
www.fantastic-four.com
www.marvel.com

FANTASTIC 4

THE FANTASTIC FOUR
VERSUS
DOCTOR DOOM

ADAPTED BY MONIQUE Z. STEPHENS
BASED ON THE MOTION PICTURE WRITTEN BY
MARK FROST AND SIMON KINBERG
AND MICHAEL FRANCE

HarperKidsEntertainment
An Imprint of HarperCollins*Publishers*

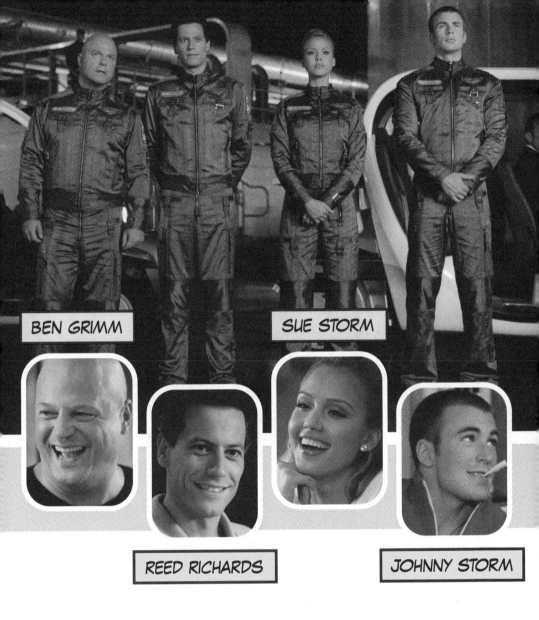

BEN GRIMM

SUE STORM

REED RICHARDS

JOHNNY STORM

Meet Reed Richards, Ben Grimm,
Sue Storm, and Johnny Storm.
They were once regular people
just like everyone else.

One day they went on a mission
to outer space.
At first everything was going as planned.
But soon their spacecraft was trapped
in a cosmic storm.
The effects of the storm changed their
bodies—and their lives—forever.

Reed gained the power to stretch his body
to amazing lengths and shapes.
Johnny could fly and create fire.
Sue, Johnny's sister, could become
invisible and project invisible force fields.
Ben became a superstrong giant
made of stone!

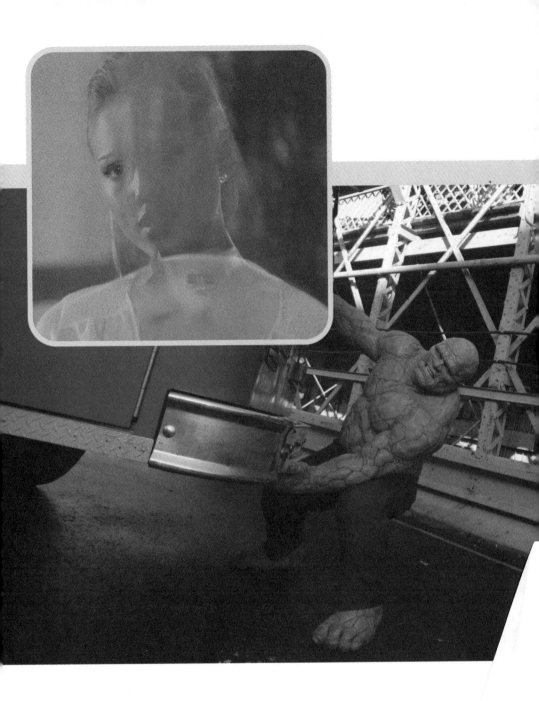

They were now the Fantastic Four!
But they were not a team yet.

The Fantastic Four would not learn to be a team until they united against the *fifth* person from their space mission: Victor Von Doom.

But first they had to learn to accept their powers.

VICTOR VON DOOM

Johnny Storm loved his new powers.
Reed and Sue did not like having
powers the way Johnny did.

Reed was working on a special machine.
When it was ready, the machine would
change the Fantastic Four back to normal,
so having strange powers *for now*
was not so bad.

But it seemed like the worst thing
ever to Ben: He hated that people
were afraid of him.
They called him the Thing.
Ben would give anything
to be his old self again.

Victor Von Doom knew that Ben was sad.

And Victor was happy about this!

He hated the Fantastic Four,

especially Reed.

He had a plan that would trick Ben into

helping him get his revenge on the group.

None of them knew that Victor had powers,
too: His entire body buzzed with electricity.
His skin was turning to metal.
He liked his power and wanted even more!

Reed's machine could make that happen. If one of the Fantastic Four used the machine, Victor could absorb all the energy that person gave off.

Victor thought Ben should be that someone. He put his plan into motion.

One day when Ben was feeling very sad,
Victor came to meet him for breakfast.
He urged Ben to use the machine.

He pointed out that the others
were away from the lab.
This was Ben's chance!

Ben was unsure at first—
Reed had said they should
all wait to use the machine
until he was certain it was ready.
Then Victor reminded Ben
how people called him the Thing.
Ben thought about how
that made him feel.
He made up his mind.
He stepped inside the machine.

Victor turned it on.

The machine drew so much energy
that all the lights in the city went out!

When the machine switched off,

Ben was himself again.

Victor had changed, too.
All the electricity collected by the machine
now charged through Victor's body.
His skin had turned completely to metal.
He was now Doctor Doom!

Just then, the others returned to the lab.
Doctor Doom zapped a volt of electricity
at Sue, knocking her off her feet.
He zapped Reed too, then took Reed
away to his compound before Johnny
could stop him.

Sue and Johnny hurried after
Doctor Doom.
They had to help Reed!
Ben wanted to help his friend too,
but to do that he needed to
become the Thing again.
Ben had a hard decision to make.

At his compound, Doctor Doom continued his plan to destroy the Fantastic Four. He launched a missile.

It was programmed to follow and destroy Johnny!

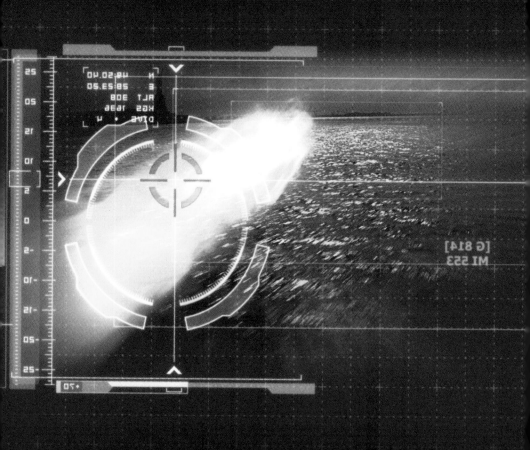

Johnny flew through the air, zigging and zagging to avoid the missile.
He led the missile far away from the city, then dove into the ocean.
The missile exploded safely in the water.

Sue made herself invisible and created
a force field to hold back Doctor Doom,
but he blasted right through it.

Doctor Doom turned to Sue and Reed
with an evil smile.

He had the Fantastic Four right where
he wanted them.

Just then, Ben crashed through the door!
But he did not look like Ben.
He had used the machine to change back
into the Thing so that he could help
his friends!
Ben and Doctor Doom began to fight
and burst through the wall,
crashed through the roof of a hotel pool,
and finally ended up on the street.

Johnny returned then too, aiming a strong fire blast right at Doctor Doom. Sue made a giant force field to hold Doctor Doom inside the fireball. Doctor Doom was burning up.

Reed decided to cool him off.

He sprayed Doctor Doom with water from a fire hydrant.

As soon as the ice-cold water touched him, Doctor Doom's blazing-hot metal body froze solid!

Working together, Reed, Ben, Johnny,
and Sue had defeated Doctor Doom.
They had finally accepted their powers.
Now they were a team.
Now they were truly the Fantastic Four!